Camilla's New Hairdo

Tricia Tusa

Farrar / Straus / Giroux   New York

To my mother,
for her love and grace

With a brush, a comb, many bobby pins, and some
hairspray, Camilla can fix her hair any way she wants.
Sometimes she looks outside for inspiration.

From her north window, she can see the wheat fields.

The south window overlooks the sea.

To the west are the hilltops.

In the distant east, there is a forest.

Camilla lives alone in a tall tower with lots of windows
but no door.

"What do I need a door for? I can see the world quite
   well from up here."

One afternoon — on her birthday, in fact — Camilla
watched a young girl trying to fly.

She was able
to catch the wind

only for a moment

before she tumbled
back down to earth.

Then, just as Camilla was about to blow out her
candles and make a wish — KABOOM — the girl
landed on her balcony.

Frightened, Camilla hid.
"How do you do, ma'am, and pardon me, please. My
name is Mozelle. I have just made a crash landing.

"If you'll show me to the door, I'll be on my way."

"There is no door," Camilla said shyly.

"No door? How do you get in and out?"

"I don't."

"How do you eat?"
"I have it all delivered," Camilla explained.

"And everything else I order from catalogues."

Mozelle took off her cap. "Wow," she said, scratching
her head.
"My goodness," Camilla exclaimed, "what lovely hair
you have. May I?"
"Sure," said Mozelle.

Camilla sat Mozelle down and paced the floor.
An airplane flew by.
"Ah-ha!" Camilla said, and up went Mozelle's hair.

Camilla served tea
and birthday cake.

Together they explored
some of Camilla's gadgets

that made the world
seem clearer, larger,
and within reach.

After a while, Mozelle said, "I've got to go. It's
dinnertime. My family will be waiting."
Camilla sadly helped Mozelle leave by way of a
tree limb.

That evening, Camilla stared out her window and
slowly brushed her hair.

Her mind wandered, and she dropped her brush. It tumbled down and caught on a branch. Camilla cried out, "What will I do without my brush?! Oh, dear! If only Mozelle were here to get it for me."

Camilla decided she would get it herself.
She tied the end of her hair to the bedpost,
then climbed out the window. Camilla was
unable to reach the brush; she got stuck.

There she hung, all night, dangling deep
in thought. Mozelle arrived early the next
morning and was quite surprised. Camilla
called down excitedly, "There's no time for
questions, Mozelle. Hoist yourself up and
pull me in. I've been thinking. I'm ready
to try!"
"Try what, Camilla?"
"Well . . . a new hairdo."

Once inside, Camilla
and Mozelle set to work.

Then they stood on the
window ledge and held
hands tightly. Camilla
closed her eyes and
took a deep breath.
"Now what?"
whispered Mozelle.
"Wait and see," Camilla
whispered back.

Wind filled the hairdo, and Camilla and Mozelle leaped into the air. Away they went, across the wheat field, over the forest, above the clouds.

By twilight, the day's wind was settling down. Mozelle
helped guide them home.

That evening, Camilla cut a door into her tower.

The next day, she opened for business. Customers
came from all over.

Some came for The Special, and some
came for something a bit simpler.

After Camilla waved goodbye to the last customer,
she set out on a long stroll.